Illness

Matthew Cash

PROLOGUE

SUSAN THE LABORATORY ASSISTANT put a three and a half inch floppy disk into the PCs tower. She spent five minutes wiping away fifteen years worth of research.

Susan the laboratory assistant put her right hand on the rubber partition and petted the white rat that sat before her on the sterile metal table in an airtight container. The feel of its soft body through her latex gloves was quite sensual. The little rodent blinked its red eyes up at her; she could see her face reflected in its innocent glance. It sat next to a small plastic box, with holes in, marked #23.

Susan the laboratory assistant reached across her left hand and carefully selected a syringe from the great collection that was laid out before her like a miniature wine rack. The syringe was marked *antivirus#23*. She pinched the rat by the scruff of its neck and slowly pushed the needle under its skin. She injected the clear fluid from the syringe into it and gently reached out of an open window and placed the rat on the ground. Susan took off her gloves. She reached for her syringe rack and selected a syringe marked *virus#23* and pushed back the sleeve of her white coat and eyed the big blue vein in her wrist.

Susan winced a bit as the needle entered her vein and felt nauseous as she injected the clear fluid into her bloodstream. She carefully disposed of both syringes, washed her hands and left the laboratory. Feeling extremely nauseous now and noticing that she had the high temperature that she was expecting, she walked into the block's staff room and sat amongst the room full of people with a smile on her face.

THE DIARY AND CONFESSION OF JACOB LEWIS

Friday 18Th March 2005. 19:03

FIRST ENTRY OF THE year. 2005 sees me two and a half stone lighter, with a slight loss of hearing and certain heightened capabilities that have changed my physical and mental self since this time last year.

In November of last year, I contracted meningitis.

I was twenty-two and weighed seventeen stone. At the start of November, the illness was discovered in the late stages, due to my uneasiness around doctor's surgeries. I had no fear of the general practitioners, just the receptionists. Evil, vile creatures that dwelled behind the sliding glass windows that separate them from the contaminated population coughing and spluttering all over the HIV and Diabetes leaflets.

I was rushed into hospital straight away in a high fever that made me delirious, family by my bedside, all in face masks; was the last thing I thought I was going to see as I slipped into a nineteen-day coma. I always used to wonder what people experience when they go into comas, was it like one long dream? Did it pass by in a flash? I've heard some people say that they could hear everything around them but they couldn't respond. I can't imagine how horrible that would be. When I was in a coma I could hear nothing, see nothing and feel nothing. I just passed out one day and the next thing I knew, I woke up feeling so incredibly weak that I could barely move.

The first thing I noticed when I came round, was how bright everything was and how strong everything smelled.

It was like being reborn.

Everything looked different, light hurt my eyes and every noise seemed to be one hundred times louder. I didn't speak for a few days; it was like I had forgotten how, the words at first seemed strange, foreign. My family kept asking me during the small episodes of consciousness that I had, whether or not I could hear them when I was in the coma, as the nurses said that they believed I could hear them. I told them I could and it was their voices that brought me round in the end. This pleased them. From the first day that I stayed awake for more than a few minutes at a time, I noticed something peculiar. It was when everyone was told that there wasn't much of a chance of me being contagious anymore, that my father took his surgical face mask off. When he did this, I thought I could see a faint grey mist like substance bloom from his mouth and nose as he spoke. It was like a cross between the visual effects that a heat haze has above a fire and what happens when you put fruit cordial into the water, how the coloured liquid churns and mixes with the clear water. It was and is hard to describe, but that is what I saw coming from my father. I never said anything, putting it down to the shit loads of drugs that I must have been on at the time.

I noticed it a couple of times a day, but not just from my father's mouth and nose. One of the nurses had it, except hers was grey with a tinge of yellow to it. Each day I was getting stronger and stronger and each day I kept putting off telling the doctors about what I was seeing. Something else I was concerned about was my hearing was slightly muffled. I did mention this to my doctor who said that it may be a result of my illness and could possibly be a permanent thing. This didn't give me much bother as it was only a slight difference and after all, I was alive! It was about two weeks after I started making a rapid recovery, that I not only could I see things that others couldn't, I started hearing things that no one else could either.

The first thing I kept hearing for a few days, was the sound of someone trying to tune in a radio, the sound of static and white noise now and again. I searched my ward and asked all of the staff who was pissing about with the radio and they insisted that they didn't allow people to have radios, only personal stereos, as not everyone wants to hear the radio at the same time. I argued with them until they told my doctor, who did numerous hearing tests on me. He told me that because my hearing had been slightly affected that the 'static/white noise' could be to do with that and it may be a good sign that my hearing might be fully restored. This perked me up a bit until I kept hearing someone saying my name.

It began as a husky whisper over the crackle of the static I could hear, just as if someone had got a radio station just out of tune. *"Jacob, Jacob Lewis? Can you hear me?"* The voice kept saying. I remember accusing everyone of whispering it behind my back, even the nurse who I had seen with the grey-yellow mist. She shouted at me, which was very unprofessional but I think she was ill as she looked so pale. Finally, after the two days of this mystery voice speaking to me, did I answer it.

I was enlightened but petrified when I found out who the voice was from. The voice spoke to me in depth once I had acknowledged its existence. Each time I answered it, it became clearer and distinguished itself to be that of a man. This man whose name is Albright informed me of what was going on.

Albright told me he was from the year 2167. He told me that he was/will be born in 2120 and worked for a company called *Salvation*. *Salvation* began as a company called *Banister Technology* situated in Singapore and was/will be a multi-billion pound company that will be established in 2023. They will specialise in radio technology.

After digital radio took over from all other radios in 2015, Kohn Banister, the head of one of the world's biggest computer manufacturers at the time, put millions into digital radio research. After digital radio reached its peak, Banister began on a new project, radio implants. In 2023 the first prototypes were ready and Kohn Banister opened up Banister Technology. After a few trials and tribulations, the company managed to install a microscopic radio into a test subject's brain. The radio could be activated just by thought and at first, there were no side effects. But after a few years of the first transmission, certain people who hadn't got the receiver implants believed they could detect the transmissions inside their heads. Another five years of testing the people who could allegedly pick up the signal without an implant, they discovered that for some reason, all of the people had suffered brain damage of some extent in the past. The majority of these people had at some point for many different reasons, been in comas.

For over thirty years, Banister researched and tried to find out why the people could pick up the signal. They never found an answer. They only found more questions.

In 2079 a man named Reagan Motherwell bought *Banister Technology* and renamed it

Salvation. Nothing was heard from the company for twenty years, when just before the twenty-second century began, Motherwell made a public announcement that would change the world.

According to Motherwell, he had devised a transmitter, that could not only transmit to the people who had suffered certain amounts of brain damage and enable them to converse back but, it was able to transmit and receive messages from people who had the same disorder over two hundred and sixty years ago!! The public thought it was nothing but a scam and there was worldwide scepticism. It took Motherwell and his company forty-five years to fine tune the transmitter and to finally prove to the world that it could do what it was reputed to do. The biggest mystery, one that Motherwell took to the grave, was how it was able to do the impossible.

Albright started working for *Salvation* in the year 2149. The depth of the work involved within the confines of *Salvation* was kept top secret, nobody actually found out what they were doing with the power they had. The answer unbeknown to the world was this;

In 2005 there was an outbreak of a super-virus which was created by a biologist who had more than her fair share of screws missing. She had created the virus and an immunization in the 1990's but had spent most of the fifteen years injecting animals of all types with the immunization. The immunization could be passed on to the animals' young and therefore making them immune to the super-virus. The biologist, Susan Davenport, after destroying all her notes and works, released the virus upon the world, herself being the first victim. She left a confessional diary which was discovered two months after the infection started.

The virus spread slowly at first, only infecting people who had physical contact with the woman, but after a few months it mutated and became an epidemic. The infected would notice intense stomach cramps on the first day of becoming infected, followed by extreme nausea and diarrhoea along with a high fever.

The vomiting would increase more into the second day and as the virus ate its way into the person's stomach. Blood would soon be brought up. On the third day, the patient would be delirious, the combination of the fever, diarrhoea, and vomiting would leave them so weak that they would be unconscious. On the fourth day, most of the people would die of blood loss or respiratory failure. The virus would wipe out the majority of the UK and Western Europe.

Saturday 19th March. 18:46

THIS VIRUS, THIS DISEASE, this homemade biological nemesis, will be released on Monday the 21st of March. Next Monday!

Albright has been 'with' me for just over two months. Being a level-headed man, I was wary of communicating with him in front of people. At first, I would mutter to him quietly, but he assured me that he had the technology to hear my thoughts. Everything has a frequency. That's what he's always saying to me in his deep husky, I think Canadian, accent. *"Everything has a frequency Jacob, everything and it's only a matter of time before we can tap into all manner of things. I believe that someday soon we will be able to contact the dead!"*

Imagine that? I believed him. I mean why shouldn't I? Who knows what people one hundred and sixty odd years in the future will be capable of? Look at how much has been invented in the last hundred years.

Once I was well enough to be let out of the confines of the Queen Mary Hospital in Birmingham, I went straight back to my flat in the busy town of Walsall. Communicating via thought with Albright proved to be difficult, virtually impossible for me. What I thought and intended to say to him were two separate things. I hate the fact he is able to infiltrate my conscious and subconscious mind. Try as I might, I could not and can not 'think' to him. My first attempts at quiet whisperings to him got many concerned glances from Joe Public and after several encounters, which I'd rather not mention, Albright suggested that I buy myself a hands-free kit. I was verily amused by this, not only because of the absurdity of it, but also the genius behind it. Often I used to make comments to my mates about how now they've invented the hands-free kit it's hard to tell the nutters from the normal people. You see people sitting or walking by themselves chatting away to apparently no-one and unless you get really close, you don't notice the microscopic earpiece and tiny microphone on their lapels. I wanted to be seen that I had one of these, so I favoured one of the larger models that fit around my right ear and curled down into a mouthpiece just to the corner of my mouth. As it had Bluetooth there were no wires.

Remember I mentioned seeing a kind of 'mist' coming from the mouths and noses of my father and the nurse at the hospital? Well after I left the hospital I noticed more people with the same. Almost everyone in fact. At first, I didn't say anything about it, but after a while, I considered discussing it with Albright. Being from the future I thought that he may have heard of such a condition, or maybe it was something to do with him. I must admit I was shocked when he didn't actually know what these 'mists' were or why I could see them. I did have a theory, the theory being that for some reason I was able to see people's breath. The main reason for me scrapping that theory, was that why would I only notice it on certain people? Surely I wouldn't. Then I struck upon what it was I could see. The nurse who had shouted at me, she had a faint grey 'mist' with a yellow hue to it. Shortly after that, she had a week off sick with a bad stomach bug. My father, a grey like 'mist' pluming from his mouth and nostrils. The next few days he was ill with laryngitis. I realised that for some reason unbeknown to me I could see viruses!

I put my theory through with Albright who said that this could be the case and he had a theory that in the future [Albright's future]

Salvation would probably discover a way to give people this gift, whether it be medical practitioners or everyone. He also suggested that it will probably be invented for me to use and by my telling Albright what I could see was probably the trigger to set up research within *Salvation* in this area. It fucking confused me. Albright explained that Time is just one big loop and that once you can master it, you can change everything. For example, if I were to go back in time to say 1989 into the bedroom of, say, a sci-fi geek and they had this idea of how cool it would be if you had a device that could change the colour of your skin at the touch of a button, I could pinch their idea and go back to the future and start work on such a device. The same could happen the other way round. I could go back to the past and tell everyone about this cool thing I had just invented in 3006 or something and then I might return to find out the 'cool thing' that I had just invented had been invented a hundred years earlier.

So basically by my ability to see viruses and telling Albright this, he would at some point tell *Salvation* and eventually, they would invent the miraculous creation and somehow give it to me now! Confused?

Anyway, I discovered I could see viruses. After Albright and I decided this was the case he kept asking me to tell him what they looked like and in what condition the people with them were in. We both guessed where this was going, why I had been given this special power. To see those who would be infected by the super-virus. We put together a detailed plan to hopefully prevent the outbreak.

Salvation had researched into the outbreak and all early cases of the super-virus and has managed to narrow the actual event to next Monday at a hospital in Birmingham. One of the many reasons why they had chosen to 'tap' into my frequency in the first place. According to Albright, the first infected were a group of seven people in a lab in a place called the Edgbaston Medical Research Centre. One of these seven people was called Susan Davenport, the biologist who had concocted and released the deadly virus. We had a detailed description of her, Albright had seen a photo of her, but as actually showing me her was impossible for Albright to do, I had to go on his description. Albright knew from the diary confessional that had eventually been discovered when it was too late, that Susan had intended to destroy all her work just before she released the super-virus. It was on a floppy disk. The only problem was that they could not pinpoint an actual time of her doing this.

Sunday 20Th March 19:21

ALBRIGHT AND I HAVE TODAY been finalising our plan for Monday, tomorrow! The idea is to get to the research centre in time to see the staff arriving. We both agree it is most probable that Susan Davenport has the floppy disk on her person, if not the virus also. What my mission is to do, is obtain the floppy disk and any syringes with the virus in, remove them and destroy them safely. Albright will instruct me on how to do this. There is no intention to harm Susan unless she doesn't cooperate.

Albright has given me the instructions on how to protect myself. I must cover as much of my exposed skin as possible. I purchased some black painters' overalls, some latex gloves and a pack of face masks from a nearby D.I.Y store. What I will have to do is soak a wad of gauze in strong bleach and place it between two of the thin face masks so as to purify any the air I intake. The mask can only be worn for a short period, five minutes max, as the fumes from the undiluted bleach I would be breathing in would be dangerous. My hands would be covered with the latex gloves, my trouser and arm cuffs will be taped down with strong adhesive tape. As my appearance will obviously attract attention, it is vital to be in and out of there as quick as possible.

To say that I am nervous is an understatement. I haven't been sleeping properly since Albright was made known to me. But on the eve before I hopefully save mankind, I am alert as ever. I keep repeating the task ahead of me over and over again. If I succeed then I will save the majority of the United Kingdom and Western Europe. If I succeed then I am likely to be arrested. I have thought carefully what I would say if, which I am bound to be, I am caught. To tell the truth would be a big mistake. I am a film fan, I know the rules. I would be certified insane if I told them I was receiving messages from a man from 2169. The story, whether it is believable or not, is to say that I am an animal rights activist and I was on a mission to destroy the work that Susan Davenport had been doing on animals. It's a pretty weak story, but it's got to be more acceptable than the truth.

Albright has made me memorise Susan's profile. She is in her early thirties, has long brown hair that will be tied into a ponytail [I think this is for Health and Safety regulations in her work]. She is pretty tall for a woman, standing around the six-foot mark. She has a buxom frame and is about a size 16. She wears black-framed glasses. And if all else fails, she should have an identity badge on with her name.

It is now 19:41, under Albright's guidance this time tomorrow I will have saved the lives of millions of people.

Tuesday 22nd March 13:56

FAILURE! FAILURE! FAILURE! FAILURE! Failure! Failure! Failure! Failure! Failure! Failure! Failure! Failure! Failure! Failure! Failure! Failure! Failure! Failure! I have murdered millions of innocent people!

Albright left me this morning. All he said was, "Oh well you're not the first to fail, we'll try someone else." I argued with him saying there must be something else I could do, but all he said in return was, "What can you do? Kill all the infected?" And then I had an ear-splitting high-pitched squeal echo through my head and he was gone. I have failed. I don't know what to do.

Yesterday morning I found a convenient public lavatory opposite the Edgbaston Medical Research Centre to change in. I put on the overalls over jeans and two t-shirts. I got the large reel of silver tape and bound it round and round from my ankles to my knees. I put on my sixteen hole Doc Marten boots. I bound tape around my wrists and put two pairs of the latex gloves on. I kept three more pairs in the pockets of the overalls. On my head, I put a plastic hairnet beneath a baseball cap. I took the face masks with the bleach soaked gauze and placed them in another pocket. Overall this, I put my long duffle coat. In the pocket of my coat was a replica gun that I had bought when I was a teenager. It could do no harm but it looked realistic enough.

I had been to the centre the night before, just so I knew where I was going to. I was amazed to find that it was in a quiet suburb. A one-storey red brick building with a small car park. The sweat was running down my body in torrents. I waited half an hour sitting in a bus shelter before anyone turned up for work. The first to arrive was a lady who I'd guess to be in her early fifties. She unlocked the building and tapped a series of numbers into the alarm system. After a couple of seconds, she was in the building. Within the next twenty minutes, five other people arrived, four men and one woman. The woman didn't fit the description of

Susan Davenport. I waited another half an hour and nobody had arrived. I studied the front of the building. I could see a lot of the rooms. Out of four, I could see that one appeared to be a staff room and the rest looked like laboratories. It was another fifteen minutes before I saw a window at the side of the building open and someone leans out. The person leant down with something in her hand. As there was no one else about, I moved across the road to get a better look. It was then I realised it was her! I caught a glimpse of her face as she put a white rat on the ground and watched it scamper away into some bushes. I knew it must have been her but I had not seen her enter the building. Surely she couldn't have been in there already?

My heart thudding in my chest I snatched the mask out of my pocket and put it on. The smell of the bleach made my eyes water so I kept it below my chin until it was necessary to put it on. Clutching my replica firearm in my right hand, I ran toward the building.

I slammed open the glass door and ran to the receptionist behind the desk which had been directly in front of me. I pointed the gun at her and told her that no one would get hurt as long as she told me where Susan Davenport was. She whimpered and said that they keep no money there. As I didn't know how much time I had, I got angry and pushed the gun against her head. If she looked me in the eye I swear I would have given up there and then. I swore at her. I said, "Tell me where Davenport is or I'll fucking shoot you-you bitch!" I hated doing it. She pointed behind her to seven doors and told me it was the first on the left. I made her get under her desk and be quiet else I'd shoot her. I pulled the face mask over my face and stormed into the room of Susan Davenport.

I saw her as soon as I got into the room. She was standing beside a work table in a white lab coat, a syringe which contained a cloudy substance in her hand. She looked shocked when she saw me. "Don't fucking move!" I instructed. I kept the gun on her as I approached her. "Put the syringe down carefully or I will shoot you," I said to her. Susan didn't move at all. This concerned me.

Was she in a state of shock? She didn't appear to be frightened at all. I had almost reached her when she spoke to me.

"You are working for *Salvation* aren't you?"

I was stunned. I stopped. "How do you know?"

Susan lowered her eyes. "You're not the first. There have been several attempts at what you're trying to do."

"What? When?" I couldn't believe it.

"The last happened five years ago. A woman broke into my home and demanded I give her the disk with my work on."

I inched a little closer. "Did you give it to her?"

Susan nodded. "But I made a copy!"

I was not expecting this at all, "Please you mustn't do this. Don't you know what the outcome will be?"

Susan laughed but there was no humour in her eyes. "Yes of course I do, the result of this virus I made," she waggled the syringe, " will practically wipe out the UK and most of Europe."

I shook my head; I could believe anyone could be so malicious. "Why are you doing this?"

"I wouldn't be doing this if it wasn't for Salvation."

"What do you mean if it wasn't for Salvation?"

Susan laughed again, I didn't notice her hand wandering towards a nearby glass beaker and I was concentrating on the syringe. "About fifteen years ago I was taken to a psychiatric hospital with suspected schizophrenia; I had been hearing voices telling me that I was going to make a lethal super-virus that would wipe out millions in 2005.

Don't you see, back then I was just a biology student with a big hatred for people in my business who experimented on animals. I had no ideas of inventing a super-virus. It was Salvation that gave me the idea! They contacted me before I even had thought of such a thing"

My mind was in knots but I could basically get the gist of what she was telling me. I wracked my brain for something to say to change her mind.

"It's not inevitable. You can change history. Put the syringe down and destroy the virus before it's released!" I begged her. I was supposed to be the one in charge, it was all meant to be so easy.

I was beginning to feel extremely ill; the fumes from the bleach were getting to me.

Susan Davenport laughed bitterly, " But you don't understand, I want to do this!" Suddenly she hurled a glass beaker at me. It hit me on the forehead. Luckily it didn't break, but it side-tracked me enough for her to move the syringe towards her arm. I had nothing to lose. I lunged at her, grabbing her syringe arm and pulling it away from her. I tried as hard as I could, but also as delicately as I could, to pry the syringe from her fingers. Susan went mad. She started screaming and slapping me with her other hand. I never wanted to use violence, never wanted to do any harm, but I smashed her in the face with the heavy replica gun and she fell to the floor. Susan lay on the floor, blood coming from her nose, with a smile on her face. I looked for the syringe. A deep penetrating chill shivered through my body, like the opposite of the effect that a shot of strong liquor has. The syringe was jutting out of her thigh, the content of which was inside her. She looked gleefully at me and said, "It has begun". Panicking I fled from the room, bolted through the small congregation of people in the reception and outside. I tore the bleached mask off my face as I ran from the building, my lungs burning, my body drenched in cold perspiration and my heart beating like a snare drum. After about half a mile I found a public toilet and went in there to change. It was then that Albright said his piece and left me.

Tuesday 22nd March 00:21

ALBRIGHT HAS RETURNED WITH good, but grave news. There is still a way I can prevent this disease from spreading. According to Albright, Susan Davenport and her work colleagues never reported the incident to the police, as Susan Davenport assured them that there was no harm done and I was just an animal activist with a fake gun and she knew that I would not be bothering anyone again. She went home early as she felt slightly under the weather. She put this down to shock, but I know otherwise. What Albright said I must do is going to take a lot out of me and I'm not sure if I am capable, but I must try. He said the only way to prevent this virus from spreading is to kill all seven of the workers by the time they leave their houses tomorrow morning. After killing them, I must burn their bodies. Obviously, I must don the horrid bleach mask to avoid contamination myself. This time tomorrow, if all goes to plan I will have blood on my hands. I will be an official serial killer, and quite possibly insane.

Wednesday 23rd March 11:56

THE FIRST TO GO WAS the nearest to me, a lab technician by the name of Ross Atkins. Albright gave me his address and I drove there straight away. I found his house easy enough, but I sat for an hour outside it plucking up the strength of body and mind to complete my task. I had a selection of knives in a shoulder bag on the driver's seat of my run down the little motor and seven bottles of petrol in the boot and some matches in my pocket and of course this diary, my confession, just in case I got caught or didn't survive. As it was in the early hours of the morning, there were no lights on in Atkins house. According to Albright, he lived alone and that it should be an easy job to do. Easy for him to say. Why did he have to choose me? Surely there are plenty of people with my condition who could pick up his signal, preferably someone with a history of violence.

I put on the bleach mask and walked up to his house. I had no idea how the hell I was going to pull this off. Security in most places was usually pretty good. I didn't think breaking in would be an option. As I got nearer his front door I noticed that it was solid wood with no peephole. This was in my favour. I stood on his doorstep shaking. My hand felt so heavy as I reached up and pressed my finger to the doorbell.

After about thirty seconds, I saw a light come on through the narrow pane of frosted glass beside the door. I heard someone rattling with the chain and knew there and then if he kept the chain on I'd be stumped as to what to do next. But Atkins, a scrawny tall man with short black hair and an over-sized mouth, opened the door looking dishevelled in a red and brown striped dressing gown which was open to reveal a t-shirt and shorts. He stared at me in my mask with a puzzled look on his face. Then a look of recognition from earlier that day ignited in his eyes and he quickly pushed the door towards the latch. I immediately kicked the door against him knocking him backwards. He fell onto the red-carpeted stairs that were behind him. Before he had a chance to move, I plunged the carving knife that I had selected from my collection in the car into him. I was sickened as I felt it slide into his chest grating against bone. Atkins screamed out in pain and begged and pleaded for me to stop. I stood horrified, transfixed by what I had done. Little bubbles of blood-spittle appeared on his lips and I saw his tongue was crimson as he cried for my mercy. Tears were streaming down my own face as I pulled out the knife and brought it down again and again until he stopped moving. Each blow causing a squeal of pain from him and a cry of horror from me.

Once he was dead, I emptied one of the three-litre bottles of petrol over him, dropped a lit match and ran before the smell of his burning flesh added to the endless years of torturous flashbacks that I would undoubtedly get.

The second was a man called Andrew Chenery. It took me forty-five minutes to get to and find his house after leaving Ross Atkins place. When I arrived at my destination I almost gave up again. He lived in a block of flats. Twelfth floor of sixteen. I took a big risk by removing my mask. Obviously, I was going to have to wait for someone to actually come in or out of the block so I could get in and I didn't think that the mask would be a good idea. The thirty-five minutes that I stood there passed like an eternity. Then at about 2:30 am two kids who appeared to be in their late teens, went up to the flat. I made some joke about losing my keys and laughed nervously. One of them merely grunted at me, the other eyed my shoulder bag and the petrol can. I got in the lift with them and had to endure the smoke from their cigarettes as it curled and spiralled in front of my face and the 'No Smoking' sign. I noticed that the smoke seemed to be thicker than usual. This was because of the virus 'mists' coming from their mouths and noses mixing with the cigarette smoke. They got off on the seventh floor and the lift continued upwards.

Albright was pretty vague on Andrew Chenery's living conditions. He didn't know whether he had a family with him there or anything useful to me. It was hard enough having to slaughter people whose only crime was having close contact with a complete psycho hell-bent on wiping out as much of the world as she could. I told my concern to Albright, "I don't want to harm anyone else, but what if he's got a family? Surely I'll have to kill them also to prevent the virus from spreading?"

Albright was silent in my head for a few seconds but then he said without any emotion, " You know the answer to that Jacob."

I knew that I must kill everyone in the flat. The lift stopped on the twelfth floor and even the computerised voice sounded ominous as it said, "Twelfth floor." Chenery's flat was opposite, number 73. I stood in the doorway of the lift and looked at the red door of number 73. Albright told me to lay something across the entrance to the lift so that I could get away quick. I opened my shoulder bag and pulled out a small knife and laid it so as the door could not shut on me. "What the fuck am I supposed to do now?" I said under my breath as I spotted that the door had a peephole. I explained to Albright my concern and he told me what to do. He said that the door would be made cheaply; would probably be easily kicked down. I put on my mask and did as he suggested I do. I rapped hard on the door and got on my knees as close as I could to the door, my face level with the letterbox. I heard the sound of bare feet slapping on linoleum as someone approached the front door. As soon as I heard the someone jangle the keys of the door, I thrust the longest of the knives I was carrying through the letterbox. I heard an ear-splitting shriek as I felt the knife go into the person. I jumped up and took a run at the door. The door didn't give on the first attempt and it almost knocked me over. My second attempt splintered the door at the lock side. By now I could hear further cries of help and the neighbouring flat door start to open. I was fucking it up big time. A white man in his sixties appeared at 72. I took a swing at him with the knife. I swear I only meant to scare him but the sharp point of the knife sliced a red line across his throat. The look on his face was that of shock as he put his hand up to his neck and saw that it was red from his gaping wound. He made a horrid gurgling noise from his throat and calmly went back into the flat and closed the door.

"Focus! Focus!" Albright shouted in my head. I turned back to number 73 and threw myself at the door. It finally gave way and more horrendous sights beheld me. Chenery was crouched beside a brown haired boy who was lying on the floor with the front of his pyjamas soaked in blood. A young woman stood with a phone in her hand crying. For a moment my vision was filled with the still pale face of the boy. Albright was going ballistic in my head. He couldn't see what I was seeing, how the fuck did he know what I was going through? Sure, he could read my thoughts but he could not see what I had done.

"Don't stall. Kill them all!"

It was then that Chenery came at me in a rage, yelling that I'd killed his son. He punched me hard in the face; I fell back into the wall. As he shouted further things at me, I saw a thick red mist rising like smoke from his mouth. The virus!

"I'm so sorry," I said as I sprang up and planted my knife, which was still covered in the blood of the old man and Chenery's son, up and under his ribcage. I pushed him to the floor and stared sadly into the face of the woman on the phone. "I'm sorry", I said again as I hit her in the face. She fell to the floor unconscious. Before she came round I brought the knife across her throat. I at least saved her the pain of having her throat cut.

I lay all three bodies together and did the deed with the petrol, then gathered my bag and got in the lift. As soon as I got outside I erupted into a violent series of vomiting and weeping. Albright was still screaming at me to pull myself together. I heard the sounds of police sirens in the background, so I hurried to my car and sped off.

The third victim was a man called David Arliss.

After I had sped away from Chenery's flat I pulled over in a lay-by and broke down. Every time I closed my eyes I could see the dead faces of the five people I had killed. Albright was at me again, sounding more and irate by the minute. It sounded as though I wasn't the only one who was losing it. If anyone had seen me in my car at that moment, they would have deemed me mad. Having screaming, shouting fits with a man from the future who was communicating with me via some yet undiscovered frequency. Albright was basically ordering me to pull myself together and complete my mission. I started up the engine, glanced at my A to Z and drove towards the home of David Arliss.

My eye caught the green neon of the clock on the car's dashboard as I turned into the road where Arliss lived. 3:23 a.m. I was not expecting to see what I saw. Two fire engines were stood next to one another. As I pulled up opposite the burnt out shell that had been Arliss's house the engines began to pull away. I quickly got out of my car and went over to a couple of morbid onlookers opposite the house. A man of about thirty and another man about ten years older. "What the hell has happened!?"

The oldest man looked very sad, "Are you a relative?"

I shook my head.

"Oh god it's horrible, about two hours ago, I don't know how, but their house caught fire didn't it, and ….oh Jesus…" He wiped a hand across his face, "All five of them died in the fire!"

"Oh no that's awful," I said genuinely upset but also, as horrible as it sounds, slightly relieved. Five fewer murders on my conscience.

I walked slowly back to my car.

"Well, that got you off that one didn't it?" Albright said sarcastically to me as I got into the car.

I was livid with him. Part of me wanted to just ignore him, but he could read my thoughts so there was no point. "What the hell do you know? How many people have you killed, hey? It's not the easiest thing to do in the world for fuck's sake!"

Albright was silent for a few seconds then he shocked me by saying, "I have killed over three hundred people Jacob. Some through experiments, some with my bare hands. But I was doing it to achieve a higher goal. What is it to kill a few people if it means you're going to save millions of lives?"

He still didn't seem to grasp the point. " What if I fail?"

"Thinking like that will make you fail. You must be positive, you must not stall. Do not hesitate. Do not think. Just kill them. You only have four left. You have come this far, do not give up now. If you do, those people's deaths will be meaningless. They will have died for nothing."

I arrived at Mark Grant's house at 4:34 a.m. I was exhausted and the sky was getting brighter by the minute. My overalls were already spotted with blood and if I didn't hurry up I was bound to be seen. When I arrived at his address, I was surprised that it was on a council estate. Judging by the other people's houses and even Chenery's flat, they had been in really good areas. This house was a semi-detached in a row of houses where almost a third were boarded up. Knife in hand and mask on, I walked up to his front door. Just as I was about to knock on it, someone opened the door. I was greeted by a skinny man with thinning ginger hair in a sweaty T-shirt and boxer shorts. He was pointing a rifle at my face.

"Put the knife down please."

I did as he asked me and placed the knife on the stone doorstep. Albright was trying to reassure me and tell me to do what he said, but to also try and get the upper hand of him A.S.A.P.

"Come in," Mark Grant ordered me. I walked over the threshold and into the small living room as instructed. He gestured for me to sit down on a green sofa. So I did.

He sat dripping in sweat in front of me. "Tell me everything!"

I was dumbfounded for a while but then asked him, "What do you know?"

He wiped one of his forearms across his forehead, "I know that you are out to harm me and everyone I work with."

"How?" I said trying my hardest to think of a way of overpowering him.

"Susan rang me; she tried phoning all of us but couldn't get through to Atkins, Chenery, and Arliss."

"What did she say?"

"She said that you were some environmentalist nutter who had some vendetta against everyone who I work with and wanted to bump us off. She told us to get out of our houses and go somewhere safe."

I frowned, "so why didn't you?"

Grant laughed with no trace of humour, "I did, and we all did. I came here to my parents' house while they are away."

"But why didn't the others?"

Grant sighed sadly; he knew then that they were dead. "They did. Atkins went to his friends' house. Chenery went to his sister's......"

Albright must have got the addresses from the police records of where the bodies were found!

"Look, just tell me why you are doing this?" he snapped at me and jabbed the gun towards me like it was a spear.

I decided to give him the 'realistic' version of events, "Susan Davenport is the 'environmentalist nutter'.

In the 1990's she created a brand new super-virus and an antidote to it. She's spent her time since 'infecting' thousands of wild animals with the anti-virus. The anti-virus can be passed down to the animals young. If the correct dosage was calculated then it could be used on humans. Yesterday she injected herself with the super-virus. Everyone she comes into close contact with will be infected with it and most definitely be dead within four days."

Grant's face went paler than it already was. Red/Pink 'mist' snaked out from his nostrils as he sighed.

"I can see you are already well on the first day of the virus. You will probably be experiencing extreme nausea, diarrhoea, and the high fever." I spotted traces of dried vomit on his t-shirt. "Later today the vomiting you are having will show the first specks of blood which will mean that the virus is eating its way into your stomach. Tomorrow you will be delirious and gradually slip into unconsciousness. And at some point the day after that, if you last that long, you'll die." I paused. "I'm sorry."

Grant was silent for what seemed like ages. Then he spoke. "What about the anti-virus?"

"She used the last of it upon a rat just before I came into the centre yesterday morning. She will have wiped all traces of the virus and anti-virus's ingredients. You understand why I am doing this?"

Grant reluctantly nodded, "But there must be something that can be done? Why is she doing this?"

"I don't know. She wants it to happen, that's why she warned you all. Told you to move so you could help it spread. If I kill everyone she came into contact with then it's the only chance I've got to stop the inevitable from happening."

Grant suddenly doubled up and clutched at his stomach and bent over the arm of the chair he was sitting in and retched. Seeing my chance I jumped up and grabbed the gun with both hands. He pushed a knee up into my stomach and tried to push me off of him, but I was too heavy. I managed to get the gun from him and he kept trying to swipe at my mask. I quickly hit him in the face with the butt of the rifle. I watched as he spits blood and teeth onto the floor. I held the rifle like a baseball bat and swung it down hard upon his head again and again until he stopped moving. I looked around the room until I found the rest of the rifle's ammunition and fetched the petrol.

As I fled Mark Grant's house, Albright congratulated me on how well I handled the incident. I told him to 'fuck off and die'. At least I had an easier weapon to use. Taking no precautions I drove at a breakneck speed to the home of the next, Janice Bolton. Her murder was the easiest. I arrived at her door at about 5:20 a.m. I knew what I was looking for as Janice was the receptionist at the centre. I basically walked calmly up to her door, put the can of petrol on her doorstep, and knocked on the door.

When she opened the door I simply blew her head off with the gun and then got out my matches. I left her body burning on the doorstep. As walked back down the path from her house I noticed the milkman doing his rounds working his way towards the murder scene. He was quite a way away and didn't seem to hear the gunshot. And the body would have burnt enough by the time he reached it. Unlike the neighbours, who were looking horrified out of their windows at me. Two more to go.

I found Rodger Dickson at 6:20 a.m lying in his bed dead. I broke into his house after nobody answered the door. After searching the whole house I found him lying on his bed. He had choked on his own vomit by the looks of things. Maybe he had had a heart attack. I don't know. The fact was, that he was dead and I didn't have to kill him. I did the deed with the petrol and was out of his house within ten minutes.

Susan Davenport. She was full of fucking surprises I can tell you.

I arrived at her place at 7:45 a.m only to find a note saying: *'To My Mysterious Masked Man, you're too late, I have a train to catch.'*

My world crashed around me then, but as I snatched the note off the door my fingers smudged the ink! She must've just left! I was amazed at how she was able to be fit enough to go out seeing as she should be in the same state as Grant was. The nearest train station was Birmingham New Street.

I knew there was no way I would go unnoticed once I got on to the train station. I wasn't going to risk wearing the face mask as it'd just make me look even more suspicious. I had wrapped the rifle up in a blanket from the car and filled my pockets with ammunition. I was going to have to rely on my extra sense to spot anyone who may have been infected with the virus. Any red mists coming from people and I would have no choice than to shoot them. It was for the sake of humankind! As I walked down the escalator, down and into the hustle and bustle of the train stations' departure lounge, the sweet smell of baking cookies and muffins wafted up my nose. Normally I would find it hard to resist *Millies Cookie Bar* but I felt as though I would never eat again. There were hundreds of people everywhere. The commuters in their business suits, newspapers tucked beneath their arms, coffee and briefcases clutched tightly in their neatly groomed hands.

Students, young pretty colourful, heavy backpacks slung over their shoulders. Holidaymakers dragging colossal suitcases behind them, always in a hurry. I didn't know where to begin looking so I just stood in the middle of the hordes hoping that I may get lucky. My main concerns were that one, she wasn't here and had left and two, she had never been here in the first place. But I had nothing else to go on. Albright wasn't being very informative. After waiting for several minutes, I went to check the platforms. Not knowing which one to check first I began at number one. The cold hit me as I went down the stairs to the platform. There were about a dozen people on there but none of them was Susan Davenport. I continued. I think it was the fourth or fifth where I saw a young man in a business suit sitting up ahead of me. I could see the red 'mist' coming from his mouth forming an interesting shape cloud above him. I hid from view and unwrapped the rifle.

This was where things got complicated.

You see as I crept up the other side of the platform, I could see another man on the next platform with the red 'mist' also. I was lucky that there weren't many people around on these two platforms, but wasn't sure how loud the sound of the gun would be. How could I shoot one without letting the other hear?

Then I had the answer.

As I stood behind the suited man I raised the gun like a club and brought it down heavily on his head. Making sure he was unconscious, I walked through to the next platform and straight up to the other infected person. Without hesitation, I took aim and fired before they had a chance to be surprised. The shot sent the man reeling off the platform and onto the railway line. After a few seconds, I heard footsteps come running down the stairs towards the platform I was on. Re-loading the rifle I watched as two security officers approached me with their hands up. Seeing no other choice I took aim again and fired again. The second officer fled for the stairs as the first dropped. I followed him as fast as I could before he could raise the alarm. He was a good few feet away from me as he ran up the stairs. He was almost at the top of the stairs and onto the busy departure area of the station when I aimed my gun for the last time. I took aim, my finger sweaty on the cold trigger. Then a millionth of a second before I would've pulled the trigger I felt a prick in my neck. Spinning around I was greeted by Susan Davenport's smiling face. I put a hand up to my neck and pulled out the syringe she had stabbed me with. It was empty; the plunger pushed all the way. Before I could do anything, she kicked me in the bollocks and pushed me to the ground. She picked up the rifle.

"What have you injected me with?" I shouted at her.

She laughed and simply said, "What do you think?"

She had injected me with the virus! It was then I noticed that there was no red 'mist' coming from her mouth. "You are not infected!"

She nodded her head. "That's right! I'm not stupid you know. I infected myself that is certain but I am not infected now. I used the last of the anti-virus on myself. I'm immune!"

"You still have a copy of the virus, don't you? And the anti-virus?"

A glint in her eyes told me yes. "I am going to the airport now, my train is now coming."

Susan Davenport said as she took careful aim and shot me in the foot. The pain was like nothing I've ever felt before. I screamed out as she casually picked up a suitcase and walked up the platform towards the sound of an oncoming train. I gritted my teeth against the pain and pushed myself up on my right foot. Doing my best I hopped down the platform after her. Looking behind me I noticed about ten policemen running up from the other end of the platform. They had seen I was unarmed and were gaining on me fast. Susan had seen me and she quickened her pace. The train was in view of the platform. I was only a few feet away from her when I lunged at her. I thought I was going to miss her, but just as I landed hard on my chest I reached out and caught hold of her ankle. She lost her balance and I watched in slow motion as she toppled over the edge of the platform and into the path of the oncoming train. Within seconds I was covered in policemen and everything was lost.

As I was carried up the stairs and through the busy station, I noticed at least half of the policemen had the red 'mist' coming from their mouths. So did about a dozen of the people in the departure lounge. So did I, it made me see everything with a reddish hue.

Now I sit writing this, my confession, my statement. Whether it is believed or not matters nothing to me at all. Within a few days, I'll be dead. I failed. Albright's last words to me were as cliched as ever, "Hmm maybe somethings you can't change."

THE END

Matthew Cash, or Matty-Bob Cash as he is known to most, was born and raised in in Suffolk; which is the setting for his debut novel Pinprick. He is compiler and editor of Death By Chocolate, a chocoholic horror Anthology, Sparks, the 12Days: STOCKING FILLERS Anthology, and its subsequent yearly annuals and has numerous releases on Kindle and several collections in paperback.

In 2016 he started his own label Burdizzo Books, with the intention of compiling and releasing charity anthologies a few times a year. He is currently working on numerous projects, his second novel FUR will hopefully be launched 2018.

He has always written stories since he first learnt to write and most, although not all tend to slip into the many layered murky depths of the Horror genre.

His influences ranged from when he first started reading to Present day are, to name but a small select few;

Roald Dahl, James Herbert, Clive Barker, Stephen King, Stephen Laws, and more recently he enjoys Adam Nevill, F.R Tallis, Michael Bray, Gary Fry, William Meikle and Iain Rob Wright (who featured Matty-Bob in his famous A-Z of Horror title M is For Matty-Bob, plus Matthew wrote his own version of events which was included as a bonus).

He is a father of two, a husband of one and a zoo keeper of numerous fur babies.
You can find him here:
www.facebook.com/pinprickbymatthewcash
https://www.amazon.co.uk/-/e/B010MQTWKK

Other Releases By Matthew Cash

Novels
Virgin And The Hunter
Pinprick
FUR

Novellas
Ankle Biters
KrackerJack
Illness
Clinton Reed's FAT
Hell And Sebastian
Waiting For Godfrey
Deadbeard
The Cat Came Back
Krackerjack 2
Werwolf

Short Stories
Why Can't I Be You?
Slugs And Snails And Puppydog Tails
OldTimers
Hunt The C*nt

Anthologies Compiled and Edited By
Matthew Cash
Death By Chocolate
12 Days: STOCKING FILLERS
12 Days: 2016 Anthology
12 Days: 2017 [with Em Dehaney]

The Reverend Burdizzo's Hymn Book (with Em Dehaney)

Sparks [with Em Dehaney]

Anthologies Featuring Matthew Cash
Rejected For Content 3: Vicious Vengeance
JEApers Creepers
Full Moon Slaughter
Down The Rabbit Hole: Tales of Insanity

Collections
The Cash Compendium Volume 1
Website:
www.Facebook.com/pinprickbymatthewcash

PINPRICK
MATTHEW CASH

All villages have their secrets Brantham is no different.

Twenty years ago after foolish risk taking turned into tragedy Shane left the rural community under a cloud of suspicion and rumour.

Events from that night remained unexplained, memories erased, questions unanswered.

Now a notorious politician, he returns to his birthplace when the offer from a property developer is too good to decline.

With big plans to haul Brantham into the 21st century, the developers have already made a devastating impact on the once quaint village.

But then the headaches begin, followed by the nightmarish visions.

Soon Shane wishes he had never returned as Brantham reveals its ugly secret.

VIRGIN AND THE HUNTER
MATTHEW CASH

Hi I'm God. And I have a confession to make.

I live with my two best friends and the girl of my dreams, Persephone.

When the opportunity knocks we are usually down the pub having a few drinks, or we'll hang out in Christchurch Park until it gets dark then go home to do college stuff. Even though I struggle a bit financially life is good, carefree.

Well they were.

Things have started going downhill recently, from the moment I started killing people.

KRACKERJACK
MATTHEW CASH

Five people wake up in a warehouse, bound to chairs.

Before each of them, tacked to the wall are their witness testimonies.

They each played a part in labelling one of Britain's most loved family entertainers a paedophile and sex offender.

Clearly revenge is the reason they have been brought here, but the man they accused is supposed to be dead.

Opportunity knocks and Diddy Dave Diamond has one last game show to host and it's a knock out.

KRACKERJACK2
MATTHEW CASH

Ever wondered what would happen if a celebrity faked their own death and decided they had changed their minds?

Two years ago publicly shunned comedian Diddy Dave Diamond convinced the nation that he was dead only to return from beyond the grave to seek retribution on those who ruined his career and tainted his legacy.

Innocent or not only one person survived Diddy Dave Diamond's last ever game show, but the forfeit prize was imprisonment for similar alleged crimes.

Prison is not kind to inmates with those type of convictions and as the sole survivor finds out, but there's a sudden glimmer of hope.

Someone has surfaced in the public eye claiming to be the dead comedian.

FUR
MATTHEW CASH

The old aged pensioners of Boxford are very set in their ways, loyal to each other and their daily routines. With families and loved ones either moved on to pastures new or maybe even the next life, these folk can get dependant on one another.

But what happens when the natural ailments of old age begin to take their toll?

What if they were given the opportunity to heal and overcome the things that make every day life less tolerable?

What if they were given this ability without their consent?

When a group of local thugs attack the village's wealthy Victor Krauss they unwittingly create a maelstrom of events that not only could destroy their home, but everyone in and around it.

Are the old folk the cause or the cure of the horrors?

COMING SOON
FROM
BURDIZZO BOOKS

THE CHILDREN AT THE BOTTOM OF THE GARDDEN
JONATHAN BUTCHER

At the edge of the coastal city of Seadon there stands a dilapidated farmhouse, and at the back of the farmhouse there is a crowd of rotten trees, where something titters and calls.

The Gardden.

Its playful voice promises games, magic, wonders, lies – and roaring torrents of blood.

It speaks not just to its eccentric keeper, Thomas, but also to the outcasts and deviants from Seadon's criminal underworld.

At first they are too distracted by their own tangled mistakes and violent lives to notice, but one by one they'll come: a restless Goth, a cheating waster, a sullen concubine, a perverted drug baron, and a murderous sociopath.

Haunted by shadowed things with coal-black eyes, something malicious and ancient will lure them ever closer. And on a summer's day not long from now, they'll gather beneath the leaves in a place where nightmares become flesh, secrets rise up from the dark, and a voice coaxes them to play and stay, yes yes yes, forever.

Printed in Great Britain
by Amazon

58281435R00061